By Jean-Luc Fromental
Illustrated by Joëlle Jolivet

BONESVILLE

Abrams Books for Young Readers • New York

There were 1,275 skeletons living peacefully in Bonesville. They each had 206 bones. That meant there were 262,650 bones.

One night in Bonesville,
Mrs. Strongbones was hanging her wash on the line
when suddenly a monster appeared!

"Help!
Somebone! Anybone!"
she cried as she ran through Bonesville.
"A monster is loose!"

Every skeleton in town
ran away in fear.

But Sherlock Bones,
     Bonesville's best detective,
          was not afraid.

"Tell me, my brave friend,
     what did this monster look like?"
          Sherlock Bones asked.

"Oh, it was bone-chattering!"
Mrs. Strongbones said. "The beast
had a giant head, a long tail,
and the sharpest teeth I've ever seen!
It ran off with my radius!"

"I will crack the case,"
Sherlock Bones promised.

The next morning, T-Bone the butcher opened up his shop.

He was busy at work when suddenly
he heard a terrible sound. It sounded like the noise
was coming from the freezer.

He opened the freezer door
and was suddenly knocked off his feet.
"Marrow me!" he cried.

He called Sherlock Bones to the butcher shop.

"Can you help me?" T-Bone asked.
"The beast stole my fibula
and now I can barely walk."

Sherlock Bones
looked around
the shop for clues.

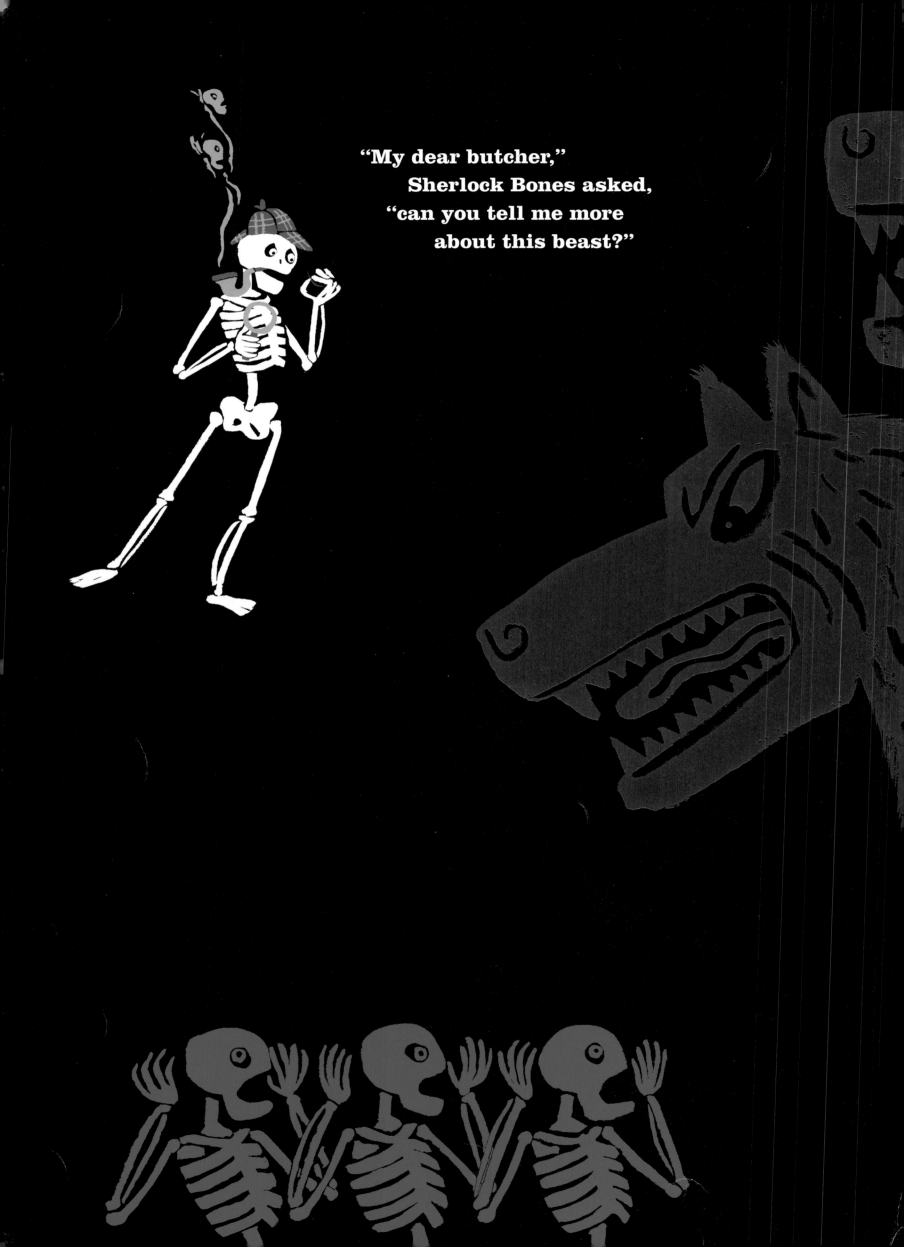

"It was a three-headed
monster that growled so loud
it rattled my bones!"

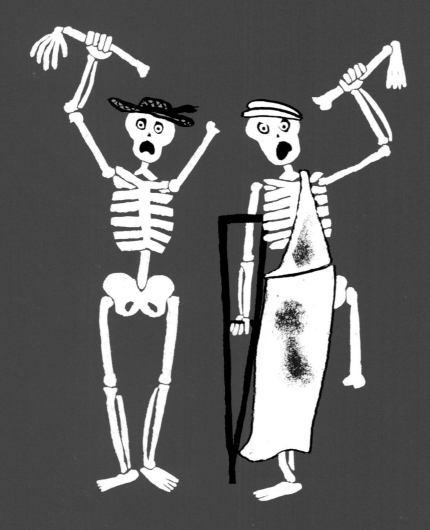

All of Bonesville was shaken to the bone.

First Mrs. Strongbones lost her radius,
        and now T-Bone had lost his fibula.
What bones would disappear next?

Dr. Crackbones was seeing his patients
at the Bonesville hospital
when suddenly he heard a crash
in the waiting room!

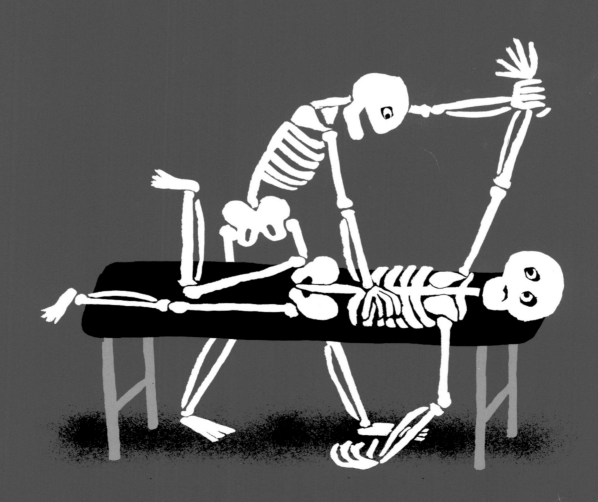

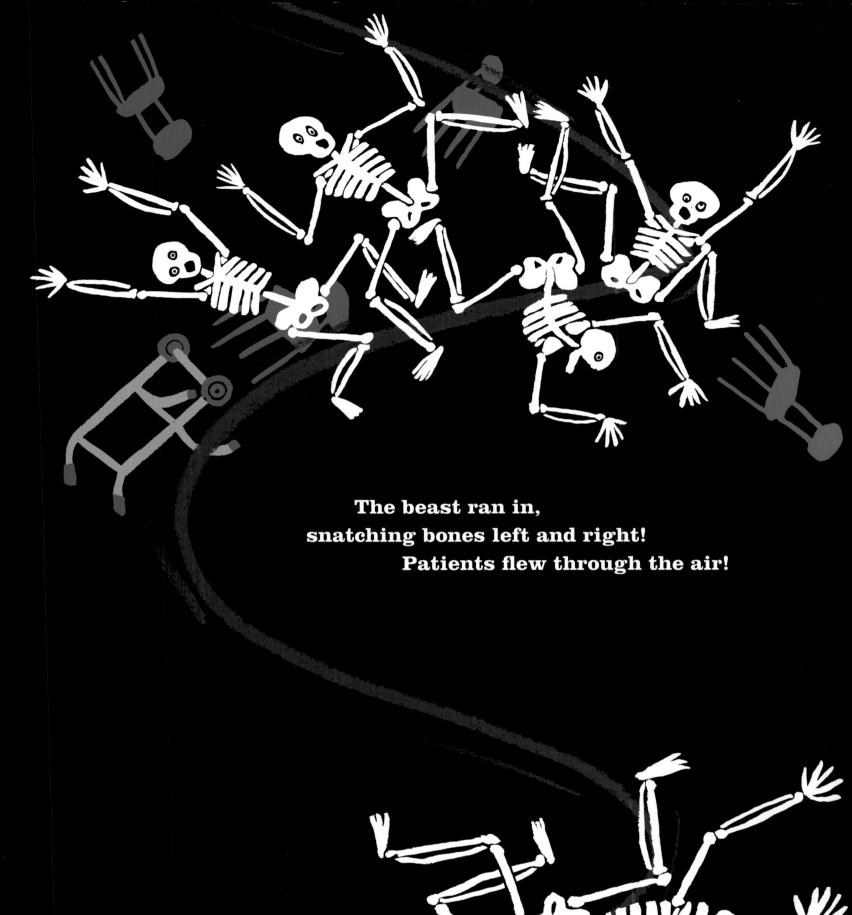

The beast ran in,
snatching bones left and right!
Patients flew through the air!

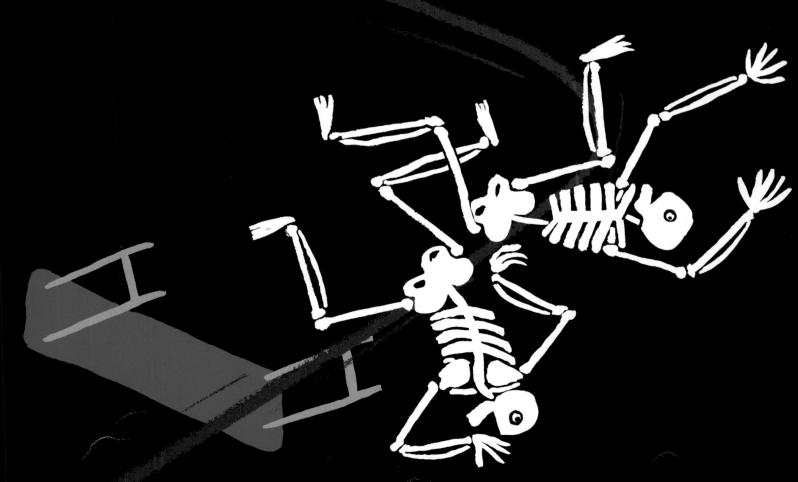

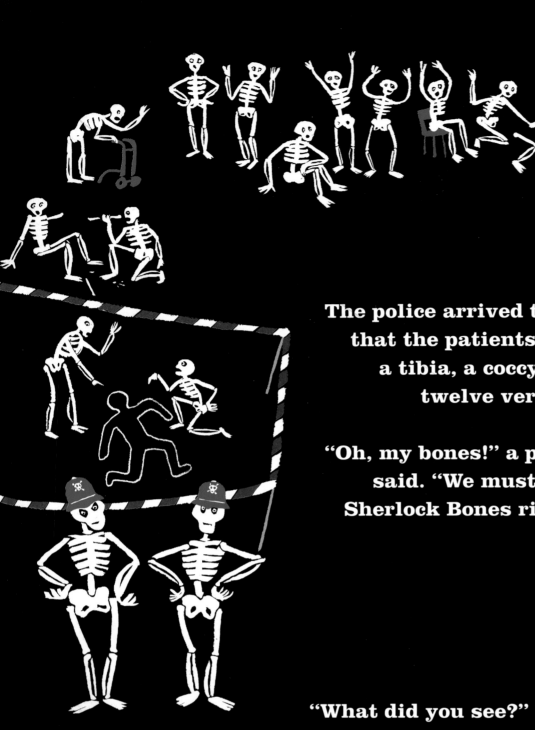

The police arrived to find
that the patients had lost
a tibia, a coccyx, and
twelve vertebrae!

"Oh, my bones!" a policeman
said. "We must call
Sherlock Bones right away."

"What did you see?" Sherlock Bones
asked Dr. Crackbones.

"The beast had enormous
wings and deadly claws,"
the doctor replied.
"It was ferocious!"

The next night,
Café Funny Bones
was in full swing.

Skeletons tapped their phalanges
and shook their pelvises
as they danced the jitterbone to the sounds of
Josephine Bakerbones and
her bonechestra.

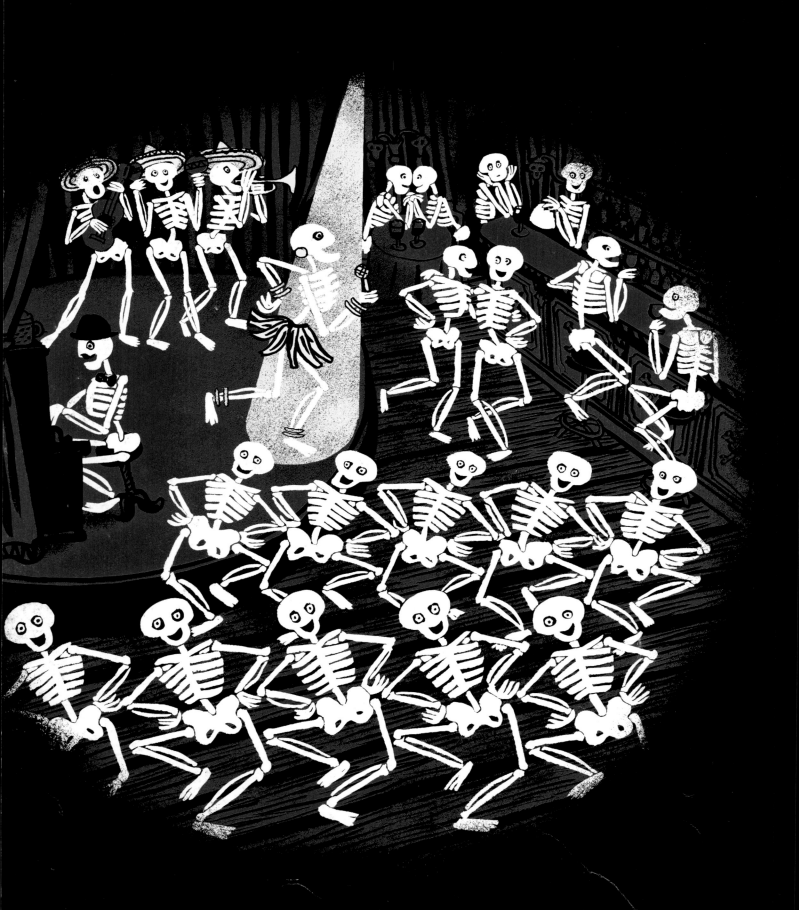

Suddenly, the beast attacked again!

Sherlock Bones rushed to the scene.
All of the skeletons had fled,
except for one.

"I lost my cranium!"
Boney the doorman cried.
"The beast had
slimy scales
and a roar that shook
the whole place
to the bone!"

The next attack was at
the local swimming pool.
As skeletons were floating
and splashing about,
the monster struck!
It stole more vertebrae,
some ribs, and even a sternum.

Then the beast bombarded
        the Boneum and Bailey Circus.

Clowns, trapeze artists,
and horseback riders
        each lost a bone in the mayhem.

During the Bone Olympics,
another ninety-nine skeletons were dismantled.

Sherlock Bones kept a list
of all the bones that were lost.

"Save us from the beast, Sherlock Bones!"
the townspeople pleaded.
"We're running out of time!
Soon none of our bones will be left."

"Be patient, my friends.
I told you I will
crack the case.
And I will, after one
last calculation . . ."

Sherlock Bones noticed that the beast took
every kind of bone, except for one.
The only one missing was the talus.

Sherlock Bones made
a startling discovery.

"Meet your monster, my friends!"
Sherlock Bones said.
"He's just a harmless dog."

The skeletons of Bonesville
sighed with relief when they saw
the friendly hound.

Suddenly, the dog ran away from Sherlock Bones
to greet a stranger who
was approaching.

"Dr. Watsbones, my old friend!"
Sherlock Bones exclaimed.
"Where have you been
these past days?
I could have used your help on this case."

"It's a long story," Dr. Watsbones
replied. "Let me explain."

"I was sailing across the sea
with some of the good bones
of Bonesville when a giant
wave crashed over us
and our bones scattered.

"When we reached land,
everyone scrambled to put
themselves together again.
That's when I realized that
none of my bones were mine!
I was made up of bits and pieces
of my friends' bones.

"Thankfully, my doggedly
determined hound,
Spot of the Baskervilles,
has now gathered all my bones
back together.

"So, here I am,
a whole skeleton
once again!"

"And here are your rightful bones,
          my friends.
Now I can return them to you!"

"Good bones of Bonesville,"
               Sherlock Bones said.
     "If you know what you fear,
                    you'll fear it less.
Your worst nightmare was
          nothing but a sweet, old dog.
Now the town will be at peace, once again."

The three friends went off into the night,
their bones happily clattering.

"We'll crack the next case together,"
Sherlock Bones said.

Cataloging-in-Publication Data has been applied for and may be obtained from the Library of Congress.

ISBN: 978-1-4197-2277-6

Printed and bound in Portugal
10 9 8 7 6 5 4 3 2 1

ABRAMS The Art of Books
115 West 18th Street, New York, NY 10011
www.abramsbooks.com